REAP THE DEAD

By

J.E. Taylor

Reap The Dead © 2024 J.E. Taylor
2nd Edition

REAP THE DEAD

**I was supposed to be Fate's bitch,
but Heaven has decided I'm theirs.**

My name's Zane Bradley, and I'm in love with a girl who is a true badass. Missy Ramsay is Fate and Death rolled up into one sexy teenage dream. And I would gladly lay my life down for her.

But Heaven wants her dead.

When the angels come for her, I make a choice. One that plunges me into a darkness I can't escape. Just like she warned me it would.

Chapter 1

*W*HAT THE HELL *have I done?*

I stare at the staff of the scythe securely clasped in my hand and then move my gaze to hers. Melissa Ramsay's wide violet eyes stare back at me with the same horror filling my soul. My heart hurts, and it's not an emotional reaction. The pain shooting down my right arm scares me just as much as the fear in Missy's eyes.

She warned me. She said I would die. Damn it all, I thought she'd be able to keep me alive like she did her parents and everyone she brought back from the dead.

At least the angels behind her have stopped their advance and seem more uncertain now. Missy didn't see them arrive, but I did. They came to annihilate Missy because she harbored both Fate and Death in her beautiful body, and Heaven just couldn't abide with one person holding all that power. That's what made me grab Death's scythe. There were simply too many of them armed with vicious-looking swords for one girl to take on, even if she *is* a true badass.

Unfortunately, if the angels have their way, there will be no future for anyone. Slaughtering Missy while she holds both roles of Death and Fate ends the world. Although I'd like everyone to believe I am sacrificing myself for the world, it's a lot more selfish than that.

I'm in love with Missy, and have been since I first saw her when we were seven or eight years old. I want her alive. I want a future with her. As odd as it seems, taking on Death is the only way I can guarantee that. That is, if Heaven isn't gunning for her just because she is unique.

Even with my motives driving me, dying sucks. My muscles clench against the pummeling discomfort. But no matter how bad this gets, I cannot let go of this damn stick. If I do, my forever with Missy is doomed.

A wind vortex circles around us, and it's like being in the center of a tornado. The mixture of salt air and the smell of rain fills the space, along with the distinct sickly smell of Death that clings to every cell of mine.

"Why did you do that?" she screams over the roar of the cyclone overtaking us.

"The world is better with you in it." I want to kick myself for how fucking corny that sounds, but it is all that comes to mind. Because declaring that I'm in love with her at this precise moment would be in poor form. My existence is better with her in it, but I don't know what the Hell my world is going to look like when this is over.

Tears fill her eyes and the book in Missy's other hand shrinks into a charm on her bracelet. Right now, I kind of wish I had the power to put this scythe on a necklace chain like she could do with a thought because it's damn heavy. I don't know how a petite girl could wield this mother effectively, but she didn't seem to have any issues with it at all. As far as the ability to shrink her Book of Fates, that's one of her new magical enhancements. She can conjure and change the physical properties of things. It's pretty boss if you ask me, but she'd give that power up just to be able to hug again. You see, when Missy took over for her parents, she inherited a nasty curse. She cannot touch anyone. If she does, she siphons their soul.

The wind whips around us, and she falls to her knees. Her face morphs from sad to a wince, like she is in exquisite pain. Her mouth opens and a scream barrels out, but I can hardly hear it above the wind and the rush of my pulse clinging to my body. Her agony ripples across her features as black smoke peels from her skin.

I want to wrap my arms around her and hold her tight, but I can't, not if I want my soul intact. And I have a feeling if I try to console her, the angels

Chapter 2

SOMETHING NUDGES MY shoulder, and the contact jars me awake. For a moment, I think I'm in the same panic room that Missy and I slept in last night. Her Papa had insisted she get sleep and the safest place in their house was that room. But it had no windows, so the blackness was just as complete as what is surrounding us now. I can't even see my hand in front of me. But then my fingers scrape on the cold, rough stone underneath me.

"Where the Hell am I?" I ask, not expecting an answer.

"The Other," a scratchy voice says from somewhere in this dark stone cavern.

I run both my palms over the rocks and the jolt in my chest has panic flushing me. The scythe is no longer in my hand. I need to find it. I roll onto my hands and knees, and start searching with my hands in frantic circles that widen with each pass. My breath wheezes as my throat closes. If I and this time, there's no Dr. Ryan to magically heal me after.

"Leave him alone," Mr. Ramsay says in a weak, sluggish voice, as if he's just coming to.

"I'll stop when he's finally dead!"

Another kick lands and the crack of ribs echoes, followed by the same debilitating pain on my right side that almost killed me on Thanksgiving.

I need to escape.

I concentrate on the shuffle of feet and lower my arms, preparing myself for another blow. I'm not disappointed. The heavy boot smashes into my arm. I move faster than I think possible and grab my old man's leg, yanking him off-balance. When he teeters over, I climb on shaking legs and turn, moving away from his muttering curses as fast as my injuries allow.

Except I can't see. I don't know where I am, or what else is in this dark cavern with me. My flight reflex is screaming, along with every bone in my upper body.

Damn it, I need light.

Brightness flares all around me, and I freeze in my tracks, squinting at the sudden bloom of light that is just as blinding as the darkness.

Missy's father sits in chains, squinting against the light just like I am. The chains anchor both his wrists and ankles into the stone so he can't

Chapter 3

FLESH POUNDS AGAINST flesh in violent succession, and grunts of pain fill the dark. I have no idea how long I've been out, but it sounds like it was long enough for my father to get sick of kicking my unconscious body.

"Stop," I whisper through cracked lips. The motion sends threads of agony from my jaw and cheek through to the crown of my head. White spots fill my vision and I think a few of my teeth are missing.

Ethereal light fills the cavern, and I squint against the brightness. A winged being crouches next to me. "Will you reap the dead?"

I blink at him like he's on drugs. "Isn't that my job?"

The angel pinches his nose and shakes his head. "Those stolen from our grip and those who are not supposed to still be alive."

I glance toward Missy's father to see another punch connect and blood spurt from between his already swollen lips. Yet he still shakes his head at me.

"Mr. Ramsay?"

"He's a little tied up right now."

Now that was a voice I'd never forget. My muscles seize as I climb to my feet. My limbs are shaking, and I turn slowly, trying to get a bead on where my father is in the dark. There is no sound, but I know in my heart where this ends. It ends with me no longer breathing.

My father wants to beat me to death. Just like he tried to do on Thanksgiving.

"Little bastard," he growls from behind me.

I spin around, right into his fist. I stumble, but I'll be damned if I go down. Because that is the end of me. His steel-toed boots are made to break bones.

Maybe this isn't the Other. Maybe it truly is Hell, because I can't think of anything more horrific than to be stuck in a room with my father for eternity.

I'm tackled full-on and knocked into a wall. My head bangs hard enough for my vision to bloom into white lights. Before I can shake it, my father punches me as if I'm a human punching bag and he's a prizefighter in training.

Each punch knocks the air from my lungs and one out of every three hits cracks something, whether it's my arm from trying to block, or my ribs. The

He reaches out and touches my forehead.

SOMETHING NUDGES MY SHOULDER, and the contact jars me awake. My skin flushes hot as I roll onto my hands and knees on the rocky and uneven ground. Echoes of pain reverberate in my head. I blink to let my eyes adjust.

I have a sinking feeling I have been here before and something awful is approaching in the dark. Panic transforms my mind into a sharp instrument just waiting for the gauntlet to fall.

"Damn it. Remember," a raspy whisper comes from near me.

Remember what?

My reflexes scream to ignore the voice, and I roll. A breeze licks my face as I climb to my feet, blind to what surrounds me. But I'm on guard now and listening for anything over my quick breaths.

Alarms sound in my head and I suddenly lean back, and that same wind blows against my face. But this time it's followed by a human growl.

My body reacts. I send a punch out with everything I have behind the force, and it connects with a body. Whoever I just slammed my fist into goes flying and the crash of flesh against

The angel smiles, and the kid closes his eyes like he just lost his last hope.

"Strike them down with your scythe and you will never have to return here to the Other," the angel says.

My gaze moves to the sadistic smile frozen on my father's face, and I nod. I can do that.

"If you falter, he will burn in angel fire for the rest of eternity." The angel points at the boy.

An instinct to protect the beaten kid in chains flares inside me. I don't understand it, but I can't seem to ignore it. "I won't, just as long as he burns." I point to my father. I want that bastard to suffer. Something deep inside me breaks, as if the last frayed thread of hope just shattered.

The angel snaps his fingers, and my father is engulfed in white flame. At first, he doesn't make a sound. And then a scream of anguish echoes on the walls, and it satisfies a deep-seated hatred in my soul.

I trade a glance with the kid. Tears track down his cheeks and he just shakes his head. The disappointment written in his features tightens my throat and makes me want to take back my agreement.

Then the angel says, "Remember your task." And he taps my forehead.

Chapter 4

MY EYES OPEN TO the black, but this time something heavy lays across my chest and I am holding a round rod in my right hand. It is quiet, and I reach my left hand out and soft fabric caresses my palm. I am not on the rocks in that cave anymore.

What's more concerning is I have no idea where the Hell I am.

When I sit up, a creak sounds from beneath me and a covering slides off my body. I remember the feel of a bed well enough and I wonder yet again where I am, although a part of me does not care at all. I'm just thankful that I am no longer in that godforsaken cavern.

I climb to my feet and walk forward as if a shadow of a memory is guiding me, although the darkness hasn't been my friend and seems to hide deadly enemies. So I hold my breath with each step, waiting for a strike from any direction. When my hand brushes a light switch, I push it up and the room lights up.

Relief sweeps through me. No one else is in the room. But I know damn well that could change at the angel's will. I run my unsteady hand through my hair and take stock of the room. There are two entries, but neither of them operates with a handle. The number pad on the wall signifies the door requires a code to open.

That kind of blows. Instead of dwelling on the inability to exit my accommodations, I focus on the room itself. The bed I woke on seems to be laden with dust, as if no one but me has been in this room for ages. Except the pile of clean clothes on the couch and the surfaces of everything else look like someone was maintaining the space. It's all very disconcerting.

I glance at the staff I'm holding and look up. The blade glistens in the light, and I raise an eyebrow at the badass scythe in my hand. This mother would have been handy to have in the Other. With one swipe, I could decimate my father and be free of that horror.

It's something I can imagine Death carrying, if Death were truly a being.

A chill skitters down my back as if someone just crossed over my grave. I shake it off and look more closely at my clothing. It's stiff and uncomfortable, as if it had dried on my body. What I can see of my bare arms looks grimy, like I had been playing in a dirt mound before I fell asleep in the bed.

A woman stands a few feet away with her hands on her hips. I have never seen a woman with a robotic arm, especially one encased in gold or brass. It's cool enough for my mind to stall. My gaze finally snaps back to her face when I realize I'm being rude by staring.

"It's about fucking time your ass woke up," she snarls and crosses her arms.

I blink at her, not taking kindly to her tone at all. "Who are you?" I grip both my towel and my scythe as my muscles tighten with the stress of the unknown.

"Mandy," she says, eyeing me in a way that makes me shift. Like I *should* know her.

I can't read anything on her face except annoyance. "Is this your place?" I point my chin toward the room. I don't dare release either the towel or the scythe.

Mandy's mouth pops open, and then a crease appears between her eyes. "No. Why do you ask?"

Caution paints her words, making me more on guard than I was before. There's only one other conclusion, and maybe she knows the codes to let me the Hell out of here. "Is it mine?"

She laughs at me and then stops when I don't join her. "You really..."

She shakes her head and bites her lower lip before asking, "Do you know who you are?"

I find I really don't know the answer to that question. My memories are filled with beatings and very little else. I remember my mother died. But who I am? That's as much of a mystery as this place is. Another memory sparks. The kid in the Other. *What had he called me?* "Z...Zane?"

She steps backward with wide eyes, and her cheeks lose their rosy color. "Holy..." She wipes her face and then runs a hand through her hair, looking completely frazzled. "What the Hell did they do to you?" Her voice shakes and she slides backward a step.

"What did who do to me?" Some internal alarms sound and my wrist of the hand holding my scythe itches. I glance quickly at it and the sigil is glowing.

Her eyes follow mine, and she takes another step away. "The angels. What did they do to you?" she hisses.

I weigh my answer as the sigil on my wrist burns. I'm not sure whether I should disclose my deal with the angel or not, but something inside me tells me I should, even though I don't think the angel would agree. But then again, the angel let my father beat the snot out of me before he intervened. "They offered me a deal."

"What kind of deal?" She pales even more and takes another step away.

I look up at the scythe and shrug. "I reap the dead."

"No shit. You are Death, with a capital D. That's your damn job. That's all our jobs." She rolls her eyes at me and seems more agitated now.

"I'm Death?"

"Yeah. You have the scythe, don't you?" She points to the rod I'm holding. When I nod, she asks, "What else did you promise them?"

The burn on my wrist nearly makes me drop the scythe. I don't know why the mark is reacting like it is, but it's pissing me off even more than this strange conversation. "They sent me to reap Fate, and all those she brought to life." I paraphrase the angel's directive, trying not to wince.

Mandy's lips draw into a deep frown and then the air pops, and she's gone.

For a moment, I expect the room to fade into the darkness of the cave. When it doesn't, I step out into the room and turn in a circle, looking for a logical explanation for her disappearance. I even look under the bed. But whatever manifestation she was, she is gone.

I rub my face and turn in a circle one more time until my gaze lands on the mirror. I could drive myself batshit with trying to figure out what just happened, but right now, I need to get this scruffy beard taken care of. Then I'll unravel this new mystery.

Chapter 5

THE MOMENT I FINISH pulling on pants and putting on the button-down shirt, my wrist burns again and the room tilts. I grab the scythe because for some reason I feel like if I'm not holding it, the world will go to shit in an instant.

I blink against the wavering walls and nearly drop to my knees at the sight of the rock cave again. My hands are empty, and my scythe is nowhere in this cave. This time the lights are on and that kid isn't anywhere to be seen, but my father certainly is there. And the bastard isn't burning like he had been when I made the deal.

He lunges at me and is stopped by a barrier that scalds his skin.

I can't help but smile. I really like the fact he's caged, especially because I am without a weapon, but that still doesn't erase the irritation scratching my skin.

The angel lands between us and stares me down. "Remember your task."

"Bullshit. You aren't delivering on your end," I snarl, pointing at my father. The fact he isn't engulfed in holy fire burns me to the core. He was supposed to be the one tortured for eternity, not kept in a cage to use as leverage over me anytime this dick of an angel expects me to do his bidding.

Darkness builds in the angel's eyes and he steps close, crowding me. "No. You need to meet your end of the deal before we will keep our word. Otherwise, I'll let him kill you over and over and over until there is literally nothing left of *you*." He jabs his finger into my chest. "Understand?"

I don't react immediately, not with the anger drilling a hole through my stomach. A part of me isn't as quick to agree as I was before. Maybe the slap of seeing my father not suffering has made me question my directive. Maybe it's as simple as waking in a place that wasn't this godforsaken cave that gave me a little perspective. Plus, wherever I had been laid out did not seem like a jail, even with the keypads.

But this place—this place is tailored to be just that. An eternal prison full of pain and anguish.

"The house you are in is full of those who require reaping. They are soulless creatures who don't deserve your mercy. Remember, they are monsters. Strike them down without fail."

I cock my head as he continues. An entire house of the walking dead. That didn't seem possible.

"Be warned, they will beg for their lives, but do not fall for their farce. Otherwise, you'll find yourself in a far worse situation than being here."

I glance around the room as doubt trickles down my back like a bead of sweat.

"Remember, Fate is a cold bitch who will try all sorts of tricks to get you to ignore your task, but she must be slayed or your eternity will be in this cave with him." He points to my father. "And that snotty kid who keeps warning you will burn instead."

I gulp and nod, vaguely remembering the person the angel is referring to. The one who referred to me as Zane. Deep within me, I feel a connection. A loyalty I don't understand. I don't want that kid to suffer.

"Anyone with blue eyes like ours must be put down. They are abominations and anyone in alliance with them must also be dealt with. They will destroy the order of the Heavens. They were revived from the dead and must be put down before the universe decides for us. Do you understand?"

I blink. "What if there are innocents in the house?"

The angel nearly growls. "There are no innocents living under that roof."

I'm still not convinced, and something tells me not to believe the angel, not without a valid reason. Doubt rubs me raw from the inside. "I thought you said to reap the dead. Those who Fate brought back. You said nothing about killing others." If I am to kill, I need a damn good reason. Being beaten for eternity wasn't enough for me to slaughter an entire houseful of people, especially if any of them are true innocents.

The angel pinches the bridge of his nose again and the buzz of the barrier evaporates. The angel disappears, leaving me with my father and his sadistic need to kill me. The lights go out, leaving me blind.

I change my stance and put my fists up like a boxer. I will not let him take me down without a fight. I'm just not prepared for him to rush me like a linebacker. He hits me dead-on and I fly onto my back. My head slams into the rock with a sickening thud. Stars fill my vision.

He lands on me, with his knees pinning my arms. One of his hands wraps around my throat and squeezes. "Little shit," he growls as he grabs a fistful of my hair and starts pounding my head against the floor. I try, but I can't buck him off.

Bright lights fill my vision as each slam of my head on the rocks jars my head until it hurts so bad I'm welcoming the darkness. But it doesn't come, just this slow suffocation accompanied by the bastard crushing my head with each terrible blow.

You'd think I'd be strong enough to throw this asshole, but I can't even wrap my legs around his body and get him off me. My eyes bulge with the building pressure on my brain from both the beating and the lack of oxygen.

And all the while, my father is laughing gleefully in the dark. How the Hell did I deal with this for so long without flipping out? An itch in the back of my battered mind tickles, but I can't reach it. Somehow, the answer is out there. I will have to dig that up right after I finish the angel's bidding.

Everything pauses and the lights come on like my random thoughts have been heard. The angel stands nearby, but the spots covering my vision don't get any better.

"Will you kill them all?" He crosses his arms, waiting for my answer.

I can't draw a breath to answer him and my head feels as though a giant stomped on it. I attempt a nod and my stomach sours from the motion.

My father is catapulted across the room, but his fingers leave welts on my throat. He lands in the area he was in when I first stepped into the cave. And I take a great inhalation, filling my starved lungs with air. I cough, and my head feels as if it's going to explode from the pressure. "At least show me what they look like," I wheeze out. Because, despite his directive, if the person isn't in his rolling deck of pictures, I'm not striking them down.

The angel snaps his fingers and a scroll of images flash. "I do not have a picture of Fate. But she is your prime objective."

My pummeled brain can't seem to keep up with the pictures, and I'm not sure I'll be able to recall them if any of the faces show up in front of me. Hopefully, my brain isn't as damaged as I think it is.

"Remember your task," he says as the pictures fade to black. "Or I will bring you back to the Other and let your feral father deal with you."

Chapter 6

MY EYES SNAP OPEN and I'm facedown on the floor. My head still throbs from the pounding in the Other. A reminder of what will happen if I fail.

I climb to my hands and knees in the same room I had been in before the angel pulled me back to beat me into submission again. I close my eyes and hang my head. What flows in front of my eyelids is the progression of pictures. Most of them have eyes that are unforgettable: bright, almost neon blue, like the angels.

For a moment, I consider rebelling. Killing isn't in my blood, but the consequences rub me like a mesh of barbed wire being dragged across my back. And it isn't my eternity that is making me hesitate. It's the strange boy burning in angel fire that gives me pause.

"They aren't human," I whisper, attempting to convince myself of my gruesome task. Squinting in the light with my throat as dry as sandpaper, I glance around the room.

Subtle differences make me straighten my back and sit back on my heels.

A new pile of clean clothes sits on the couch and the light in the bathroom is off. I could have sworn I hadn't turned it off when I stepped out into the room. And I certainly hadn't made the bed. Especially with clean linens.

But the oddest thing beyond that is the bottle of water on the table, like whoever neatened up the space figured I'd be thirsty when I woke. They aren't wrong, but it still is creepy as hell.

I slowly stand and glance around with my scythe still gripped in my hand. I stare at it like it's as foreign an object as anything else in the room. I wonder why it didn't come with me to the Other if it was in my grip here. No solid answer comes, so I cross to the bathroom and flip on the light because I dislike dark spaces.

It reminds me too much of the Other. The dirty pile of clothing is gone from where I had left it. I hadn't folded the towels, but they were neatly folded just the same. I lean over and take a whiff of them. They smell freshly laundered. A chill captures me at the thought of those faces caring for the room while I lay unconscious on the floor.

The air shimmers again and that figure who had surprised me outside the bathroom materializes. I stare at her, suspicious that perhaps she had been the one to neaten up the space. I don't get that from her at all. Frankly, she seems more battle-ready soldier than homemaker.

"Are you on the side of Heaven?" I ask, because I can't side with someone that has opposing allegiances.

She laughs at me. "Oh, Hell no."

The tattoo on my wrist burns and pain lashes through my head. Anyone not on Heaven's side is my enemy. I'm not sure whether or not that is my thought, but it is all I need to react. I swing the scythe. Mandy lifts her metal arm in defense and my scythe violently bounces off it, nearly throwing me on my ass.

I swing again, but before the blade reaches her, she blinks out.

"Come back here and fight!" I bellow at the ceiling, spinning around with my weapon at the ready.

The creak of the door catches my attention and I spin around, angry that I didn't take out that creature when I first saw her. But the blue eyes that peer through the door catch me off guard, and the face in one of the pictures appears in the crack.

His eyes widen at the sight of me.

I charge, raising the scythe, but the door slams closed before I can cross the distance. I swing anyway, burying the blade into the door. I yank it out and swing again. But no matter how many times I strike the wood, all it does is surface damage, as if the core is unyielding steel.

My blade doesn't break through, even though the sting from the sigil on my wrist demands I strike.

I dislodge my blade and pace across the space, cursing loudly as the blaze in my wrist poisons my mind. I need to get out of this room. I need to satisfy my end of the bargain. Otherwise, I am as doomed as I feel right now.

Chapter 7

I FINALLY CALM DOWN enough to position myself to the side of the opening, waiting for the next opportunity. Just when I think I missed my chance, the door creaks open. I hold my breath, waiting for it to widen enough for me to slip through. I catch his profile as he sticks his head inside the door, and then I burst through the opening before he can shut me back in.

Freedom gives me a rush of strength and my forceful exit knocks the man to the ground. He stares up at me with those wide, ethereal blue eyes and scrambles to his feet. My sigil brightens. This is one of the dead I have to collect. Even if I hadn't recognized his face from the slide show the angel showed me, I'd still need to cut him down.

Everyone in this house needs to be dealt with. Now. Sending them back to Heaven will sound alarms, and Fate will come running right into the edge of my blade.

I swing my scythe and it whistles through the air, hitting him at the crown of his head and slicing down as if he's made of butter, not bone. Nothing happens at first and then two halves fall to the ground. His eyes are still open and wide, as though he never felt his death.

I expect a ghost or a soul to come out of him, but nothing does. Just like the angel promised. These things weren't even human, and that fuels my need to destroy them.

"Run!" a scream follows.

I turn, swinging with righteousness, and my blade severs a petite blonde's head, and it rolls across the floor. Blood plumes all over the front of me from her headless body. A moment later, the body crumples to the ground as if it just realized it was dead.

The same absence of a soul grips me and catapults me forward.

Two kids bolt up the stairs at the far end of the room, screaming. Before I make it halfway across the room, a man appears at the bottom of the stairs. White wings fan out from behind him and light as pure as I've ever seen shines through him.

But his face is one of the souls I must reap.

I step forward and hit a solid wall that sends a healthy shock through my body. I leap backward and nearly slip on the slick puddle of blood seeping into the carpet. The sting of it sizzles on my skin and I glare at the angel-like creature.

A blonde appears from the stairwell. Another face I have been called to reap, except her eyes are not blue like the neon ones that flash from next to her. Her brown eyes are soft with fake concern.

"Don't hurt him. She will never forgive us." She sticks her hand out like a stop sign. "Calm down, Zane."

The angel from the Other told me this would happen. He said they would all beg for my mercy, but I was not about to listen. I cannot be swayed by whatever argument they try to launch, and the burn in my wrist is a stark reminder of my task.

I just hope their deaths will bring Fate to me. I want that bitch dead by my hands, preferably squeezing the life out of her. Again, the thought seems foreign inside my head, but I shake it away.

I step forward again into the electrified barrier and hiss as I jump back. The jolt hurts all the way to my teeth.

"Go," the blonde tells the angel. "Get them out of here." She nods toward the upstairs. "All of them."

I can't help but wonder how many more of the faces are in the house right now. My wrist twitches, scraping the scythe along the invisible fence caging me in. The shock isn't quite as bad through the metal, as if it is absorbing the energy instead of being scarred by it.

He glances at the blonde with a headshake. "Not until he's dealt with. I can't hold him in place indefinitely, especially at a distance."

"I'll be fine. I need to find out what happened with Nick. Now go, before Michael gets home and finds this." She waves at the dead soaking the carpet red.

Before the man leaves, he sends a glare in my direction and turns, bumping into a brunette barreling into the room like the place is on fire and her favorite puppy is lost in the corner.

When her lavender eyes land on me, a jolt as strong as the electrified wall zaps me, and it feels like my heart stops in my chest. For a moment, I can't draw a breath and I know deep down that this is who I've been waiting for. This is Fate, and she is as breathtaking as the angel warned.

My body reacts to her in a way that surprises me. I want to kiss her. Hell, I want to fuck her, but I know better. This is part of Fate's cruel trick.

"Go," she says, but her eyes are glued on me. When the man doesn't budge, she actually turns and pushes him. "Go!" she yells in his face, and points upstairs.

His jaw tightens, and then he marches out of the room.

"You, too, Mom," she says to the little blonde. And now I see some resemblance in the shape of their noses. But the black hair doesn't match, and neither does the age. They look maybe a year apart at best.

"I need to find out what happened to your father." The blonde turns to me. "Did you see Nick?"

I growl in response and test the barrier in front of me, yanking my hand away from the zap. But I welcome the shock. At least it puts me back into control and my entire body buzzes.

The barrier doesn't feel as strong as the first time I walked into it, and I wonder whether the number of times I've tested it has weakened it. Maybe playing this game of test and jolt with the force field is doing just that. I do it again just to be sure and this time the sting travels all the way up my arm but stops there.

"He has dark hair like Missy"—she points at the violet-eyed woman—"he has blue eyes, and probably still looks like he's eighteen?" she asks with a hopeful lilt to her voice.

I stare her down and test the barrier again, this time with the edge of my scythe to avoid the shock. The barrier crackles on contact. Although the blonde steps closer, the dark-haired vixen hangs back, studying me as if she doesn't believe what she is seeing.

"What? You've never seen Death before?" I snap at her and bang the scythe against the barrier again for show. I'm not even sure whether I should trust Mandy's explanation of who I am, but it's worth a shot. I want this woman to shake in fear at the sight of me.

She huffs. "I was Death before you stupidly ripped that scythe out of my hand ten years ago."

I cock my head. She can't be serious. Why would anyone *choose* to be Death? Least of all me. Besides, *she* is someone I would remember. I burst out laughing. "Bullshit."

She presses her lips together and her eyes actually gloss over with unshed tears, which surprises me because Heaven said she was a crafty and cold bitch. Her devastated look does not fit their description at all.

"We thought you might say that." She turns to the stairs and nods at someone I can't see.

An older redhead steps onto the landing with her fingertips sparking, and her picture flashes in my memory. She has the same ethereal blue eyes as the first idiot I cut down and the man with the white wings. Except the difference with this one—she has fiery wings.

Either way, she is also on Heaven's hit list. I blink and then narrow my eyes. This must be the devil's daughter that Heaven expects me to terminate. But the barrier is still a little too strong for me to break through without serious damage. I test it again, actually enjoying the shock that travels into my arms. It makes the sigil on my wrist glow as brightly as their eyes.

The redhead levels a wide-eyed stare, blinking rapidly as she scans the carnage around me as if she cannot believe I am capable of such destruction. She will learn the truth once I escape. She trades a quick glance with the one the blonde called Missy.

"We'll deal with the ramifications later. He needs to see," Missy whispers softly, as if the comment was not meant for my ears. But I'm tense enough to pick up every sound, even their flitting heartbeats pounding out their underlying fear.

The redhead inhales and then blows out of her mouth and nods. She closes her eyes and turns her palms toward me. The space between where she is standing and the barrier I am caught behind ripples and then morphs, capturing my full attention.

The sky is streaked with pinks and purples of a sunset. The ocean sits in the distance beyond an expanse of lawn broken by a pool and then a rock wall separating the grass from the deep, tumultuous ocean. A teenage girl stands on the grass with her back to us, with what looks like an ancient book in one hand and the scythe in the other.

The same scythe I'm gripping right now. Something about her stirs a need deep within me, and I nearly growl at myself.

The view switches from the girl outside to inside a house where many people are watching her. Every single one of them I recognize from the images the angels showed me. Every single mortal who must meet their maker today.

A ruckus pulls my attention to near the sliding glass doors, and a much younger version of me is struggling with a black-haired kid. He is attempting to stop me from going outside to the girl, and I deck him. My throat closes as I get a full view of the kid on the ground.

He is the same one my father threatened to kill in *the Other*. A sharp pain pierces my head, and I close my eyes for a moment. My wrist heats and I want to shake it, but the scythe is still in my grip.

Instead, I refocus on my younger self, who utters a half-hearted apology and closes the glass door behind him. He is unsure in his gait as he approaches the girl, as if he's afraid of her. Something makes her turn toward him. Her eyes carry a hint of fear, but it quickly turns into irritation as she glances toward the house and then back at the younger me before she juts her chin toward the house.

That's when I see them.

A swarm of angels. Thousands of them landing en masse on the grass and hovering over the water in the distance. And every single one of the winged bastards wears a scowl as they come toward us. I can only assume their intent is to wipe us all out. Me included. And that's the only logical reason I can think of as to why I grab the scythe from the girl.

No sooner do I have this weapon in my hand than a whirlwind swirls around the two of us in the yard, blocking my view. When it subsides, the girl is on her hands and knees, sobbing. My body is prone on the ground, with the scythe crossing my chest. Which is exactly how I woke up in the dark room I just escaped from. My chest is still, and my face beyond pale. I'm gray and I recognize the face of death.

The vision fades and I stare at the empty space, blinking. If what I am being shown is the truth, then Missy wasn't lying when she said I took the scythe. But the thing is, I have zero recollection of any of those events. I'm skeptical as I glare back at the three women. For all I know, that could have been a well-orchestrated hallucination peppered with just enough truth to make me buy it.

"You can go now," Missy says to the redhead.

"I love you, Missy. Be careful," the redhead says softly and gives her a hug. And then she flees up the stairs, out of sight.

I jolt at the sudden loss of one of my quarries, but there are still two in the room who I need to run my blade through. Missy is my primary target and the bitch Heaven warned me about. They said she'd try to trick me. They weren't fooling.

"The one you punched is Nick. Did you see him at all?" the blonde asks as she approaches.

I glance over her head at Missy and then back at her. Her eyes don't look like a monster's eyes, and for a moment, I doubt my mission. But then I remember: none of these monsters have souls. I lick my lips and give the slightest of nods, hoping she will close the gap for more information.

"Is he okay?" She steps closer. Just outside the barrier, looking up at me with imploring eyes.

Before she can move out of my reach, I turn my scythe and shove the pointed end right at her heart. "You can see for yourself," I snarl.

I don't know who is more surprised when it actually impales her, but I don't have time to pull it out when a wave of power knocks me clear across the room.

This time, an orb of white light surrounds the blonde. And I stare at it in awe, swallowing the doubt as the manifestation of her soul seems to form. The others didn't do that. They just ceased, like Heaven promised.

Movement captures my attention. Missy is charging at me and I'm on my feet, ready for her, tossing my doubt aside. Her hair whips as she moves and when she jumps into the air to execute a roundhouse kick, I shift my weight in time to avoid her foot slamming the side of my head. But she's now within reach and I grab her as she lands, knowing my touch is as deadly as my scythe.

I slam her against the wall and my hands wrap around her slim throat, squeezing. Her knee comes up between my legs with enough force for me to lose my grip for a moment, but the dull ache between my legs fuels my vengeance.

She's a fighter, and I lean my body against hers as she struggles and scratches my arms. But that's as far as she can get with the way I have her pinned. Her gasps and wheezes tell me she's still getting air and I press harder.

The horror in her eyes is mixed with something else, something I don't recognize until a tear escapes both eyes. It's the same look of heartache and betrayal I once saw on my mother's face when she caught that lying bastard cheating on her. The echoes of her sobs still give me nightmares, more than her deathbed goodbye.

A ding emits from Missy's wrist, and I stare at the charm bracelet as she pounds on my arms.

My gaze jumps to hers as my head feels as if something inside explodes. A flood of memories bursts forth through the prison that Heaven manufactured in my head. Like a picture show on steroids, the images flash through my brain. Not only images of this girl saving me in every way possible from the first moment I met her, but to the duplicity of Heaven's horrors.

I loosen my grip, but the damage is already done.

"Zane," she gasps.

"Oh, Melissa," I whisper, and my thumb passes over her lower lip. It blackens under my touch and I curse the gods. Tears fill my eyes as I finally recognize the woman I would die for.

Correction, the one I *had* died for.

And I am responsible for doing the thing I vowed never to let happen.

I am stealing her life with my touch.

I have to stop this.

She cannot die.

I don't care what the consequences are. I lean forward, capturing her mouth with mine. If she could wish life back into the dead, so could I, right?

She kisses me back with a sob, but then she goes slack, and I catch her, holding her to me as I fall to my knees.

My chest feels flayed open and my heart pummeled like it's been tap-danced on by a legion of reapers. I close my eyes and rest my forehead on hers, shaking from the realization that I just delivered her to those bastards on a silver platter.

"I'm so sorry, Missy."

I rock her as my tears fall onto her face. I press my lips to hers, wishing life even though I know deep in my soul I don't possess the kind of magic she does.

She wheezes out her last breath with my name on it and then stills in my arms. Her chest no longer moves and the feral beast Heaven created resurrects inside me, except it isn't aimed at their targets anymore.

Another ding comes from her wrist, and I bellow a wordless scream at the ceiling, vowing to kill every last goddamned angel in Heaven.

The End

Continue the series with KISSING FATE, the last installment of THE DEATH CHRONICLES II

ABOUT J.E. TAYLOR

J.E. Taylor is a USA Today bestselling author, a publisher, an editor, a manuscript formatter, a mother, a wife, a business analyst, and a Supernatural fangirl. Not necessarily in that order. She first sat down to seriously write in February of 2007 after her daughter asked:

"Mom, if you could do anything, what would you do?"
From that moment on, she hasn't looked back.

Besides being co-owner of Novel Concept Publishing, Ms. Taylor also moonlights as a Senior Editor of Allegory E-zine, an online venue for Science Fiction, Fantasy and Horror, and co-host of the popular YouTube talk show Spilling Ink.

She lives in New Hampshire with her husband and during the summer months enjoys her weekends on the shore in southern Maine.

Visit her at www.jetaylor75.com to check out her other titles and sign up for her newsletter for early previews of her upcoming books, release announcements, and special opportunities for free swag!

If you liked GRIM'S DAUGHTER, you should check out the rest of the books in THE DEATH CHRONICLES II:

THE DEATH CHRONICLES II

Death is the family business, but not one I want to pursue. Thankfully, it's been passed down from father to son for generations, so it should skip me as Death's daughter. Then I won't have to stop being alive and can actually live my life. Right?

Well, the reapers don't agree. And neither do the angels.

One thinks I'm destined to take over, the other believes I will destroy existence. Both want me dead to match their own agendas.

I have an agenda of my own, and Leviathan who has sworn to protect me. But once my family and friends start being targeted, the family business, while grim, might be the only choice I have to save those I love.

You might also like these other titles set in the same world as THE DEATH CHRONICLES II:

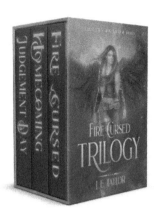

FIRE CURSED TRILOGY

Lucifer's daughter rises.

Faith Kennedy's mother hid the awful truth from her daughter for sixteen years. Until she lay on her deathbed. Only then did she reveal who sired her daughter, and the revelation terrifies Faith.

The devil may have sired her, but he only wants her beating heart ripped out of her chest. After all, that's where her angel grace fueling her fire power is stored, and that will give him what he needs to bring about humanity's fall.

And Lucifer will take down anyone who gets in his way.

When Faith is given an ancient knife that can kill the devil, she faces the toughest challenge of her young life. She must hunt Lucifer and put him down. Otherwise, the world will burn.

But if she succeeds, she may wipe herself, and everyone she loves, out of existence.

This set includes Fire Cursed, Homecoming, and Judgement Day.

RUNNING FROM THE DEVIL TRILOGY

An escaped demon and a snarky cat face off against the seven deadly sins.

Escaping from Hell was just the beginning of Phoebe's problems. In Hell, she had a position of legend. A marquis of torture. But on the human plane, she is just another New York City destitute.

Before she has a chance to get her bearings on the unforgiving streets, Fate steps in and offers her a chance at redemption, but it doesn't come cheap.

She must bring in the demons that escaped alongside her while making sure no humans are harmed in the process. In order to do that, she needs to learn to live in the human world with the help of another one of Fate's parolees, a snarky cat named Smoke.

If it means never seeing the halls of Hell again, Phoebe will do anything, even battle the seven deadly sins single-handed.

Find these titles and other fantasy
and suspense titles on J.E. Taylor's
website!

www.JETaylor75.com